The diary of

A YOUNG ROMAN SOLDIER

Editor Louisa Sladen
Editor-in-Chief John C. Miles
Designer Jason Billin/Billin Design Solutions
Art Director Jonathan Hair

Text © 2000 Moira Butterfield

The right of Moira Butterfield to be identified
as the author of this work has been asserted.

First published in 2000
by Franklin Watts
96 Leonard Street
London
EC2A 4XD

Franklin Watts Australia
14 Mars Road
Lane Cove
NSW 2066

ISBN 0 7496 3661 0 (hbk)
0 7496 3942 3 (pbk)

Dewey classification: 937

A CIP catalogue record for this book is available
from the British Library.

Printed in Great Britain

The diary of
A YOUNG ROMAN SOLDIER

by Moira Butterfield
Illustrated by Brian Duggan

W
FRANKLIN WATTS
NEW YORK • LONDON • SYDNEY

ALL ABOUT THIS BOOK

This is the fictional diary of Marcus Gallo, a young Roman legionary stationed in Britain between AD59-61. He is a twenty-year-old soldier who has just finished his training. Now he's being sent to reinforce the troops already in Britain.

The Roman Army was made up of legions, like regiments in a modern army.
Every legion had its own name and number and was split into groups like this:

A Legion =   about 5,000 men (10 Cohorts)

A Cohort =   480 men (6 Centuries),
except for the First Cohort,
an extra-big group of 800 men

A Century =   80 men (10 Conturbeniums)
with a Centurion in charge.

A Conturbenium = 8 men

In this story you'll be joining in the lives of Marcus Gallo and the other men in his conturbenium. He belongs to a legion called the Twentieth Valeria (written by the Romans as XX Valeria).

We cheated! (but for good reasons).
● A soldier like Marcus would have spoken and written in the Latin language. We have written in English, so you can understand it.

● In real life nobody has ever found a diary of a Roman soldier, but we do know some of the history of the time. We don't know the exact dates of marches and battles, but we do know roughly when they happened.

We count years from the birth of Christ, but Marcus probably wouldn't even have heard of Jesus. He couldn't have used BC ('Before Christ's birth') or AD ('Anno Domini', which means 'the Year of our Lord' in Latin). We've used them to make the timescale clearer for you.

MARCH 14TH AD59
ARMY FORTRESS IN GERMANY

The noise in this barrack room is driving me crazy! I feel like shouting out loud, but I'd wake the other soldiers in here, so I'll just write it in my diary and hope it makes me feel better.

STOP SNORING!

It's all right for them, sleeping like babies on their bunks. I'm wide awake and the sun isn't even up yet. I might as well be on night-time sentry duty.

There's a rumour that we'll soon be off to Britain to meet some screaming bloodthirsty locals. If I don't get some sleep, I'll be screaming too.

March 15th ad59

"Marcus Gallo, you lazy excuse for a soldier! Stop yawning and move yourself!"

Every morning it's the same. Our cuddly Centurion Sejanus marches round all the barrack rooms in his century shouting at us to get up. If he knew I'd called him cuddly he'd have me on toilet-cleaning duty for days. Actually, he's about as cuddly as a wild lion is to a gladiator.

THE BOYS IN MY CONTURBENIUM

LUCIUS

MARCUS – GOOD-LOOKING HERO (THAT'S ME!)

GAIUS

MARIUS

FELIX

OUR DEAR CENTURION SEJANUS

PETRUS

GALERIUS

LEPIDUS

March 16th AD59

Weapons training today. As we attacked the wooden practice posts with our blunt swords Marius moaned under his breath about having to practise the same fighting moves over and over again. One day Sejanus will hear him and give him a whack with his centurion's stick for complaining.

We're all trained in the same way, every last Roman soldier in the Roman army from the deserts of Africa to the bogs of Britain. Centurions shout at us wherever we are.

"When you're facing the enemy this is what you do… Listen at the back, you horrible lot!"

"One. Throw your first javelin. Two. March closer and throw your second javelin. Three. Advance on the enemy, holding your sword in your right hand. What hand did I say, soldier?"

"Right hand, sir."

"Four. Hold your shield and use it in your left hand. What hand did I say, soldier?"

"Left hand, sir."

"Use your shield to bash the enemy, and stab low with your sword. If you lose your sword, use your dagger."

"What do I do if I lose my dagger, sir?"

"You die for Rome, boy."

Sejanus always shouts the same thing over and over again in weapons training:

"Stab low! Stab low! Hit the enemy where it hurts!"

I sometimes hear those words in my sleep.

Thank Zeus I am getting some rest now. I've found a way to block out the snoring in the barrack room, by wrapping my cloak around my head in bed.

MARCH 18TH AD59

All the troops in the fort were lined up in front of the main headquarters to hear a speech by the commanding officer. He told us we'll be going to Britain to reinforce the troops under the new governor, Suetonius Paullinus, and then he sacrificed a goat to get Mars, the god of war, on our side. A few of the native British Celts don't like being part of the Roman Empire and they want to send us Romans back where we came from. We're going to show them who's in charge and teach them a fighting lesson they will never forget.

MARCH 19TH AD59

Today it's Quinquatrus, the day that marks the start of the Roman fighting season. I'm feeling excited and scared at the same time. Ever since I joined the army at eighteen I've wondered what it would be like going to war. All through my training, while I was learning to build, dig, swim, and all the other things a Roman soldier has to do, I wondered whether I would ever have to actually fight in a battle. It looks like I'll be using my sword for real pretty soon.

MARCH 20TH AD59

Last night I dreamt I was in front of an enemy
army on my own! I threw my javelins, one after
the other. Then with awful shrieks the enemy
came running at me. I bashed one of them with
my shield and attacked another with my sword,
desperately stabbing faster and faster.

"Stab low! Stab low!" I didn't know it but
I was saying the words out loud in my sleep,
and I woke Lucius. "Oi, Marcus, dream about
something quiet, will you?" he muttered.

MARCH 21ST AD59

Gaius asked what Britain was like and because
he is the youngest one of us the others thought it
would be easy to make him feel scared.

"I've heard it's misty and boggy."

"I've heard it's haunted."

"It's wet and cold," came the replies, though
none of us have actually been to Britain yet, only
heard about it from other soldiers. It's got lots
of precious metal that we can mine, so the
Empire wants it and that's that. We're going to
keep it.

Petrus seems to know everything (or thinks
he does). He explained that the Emperor Julius
Caesar went to Britain first but didn't stay. Then
the Emperor Claudius sent a whole lot more
troops there and now it belongs to Rome. Well,
not quite. We've only got the southern part of
the country, but we'll get the rest soon.

Felix said he'd heard the Celts make human sacrifices. Gaius gulped and I guessed what was coming next. Sure enough, Felix leant forward and began to tell the true story that strikes fear into every legionary – the blood-soaked tale of Varus and the lost legions!

It goes something like this...

WE ALL KNOW HOW GOOD THE ROMAN ARMY IS AT BATTLES BUT WE'RE NOT QUITE SO INVINCIBLE WHEN IT COMES TO BEING AMBUSHED, AND OUR ENEMIES KNOW IT. YOU ONLY HAVE TO THINK OF THE TIME WHEN QUINTILLIUS VARUS LED THREE LEGIONS INTO A GERMAN FOREST...AND NEVER CAME OUT.

AT FIRST NO ONE KNEW WHAT HAD HAPPENED, WHY MORE THAN 15,000 ROMAN SOLDIERS HAD DISAPPEARED WITHOUT TRACE....

IT WAS ONLY LATER THAT SEARCH PARTIES DISCOVERED THE SCENE IN THE SHADOWY SWAMPS. AN ENEMY ARMY HAD BEEN HIDING IN THE TREES AND AMBUSHED THE LEGIONS WHILE THEY WERE BUILDING A CAMP.

ROMAN SKULLS WERE FOUND FASTENED TO TREE TRUNKS, BONES WERE PILED UP WHERE SOLDIERS HAD FOUGHT TO THE DEATH AND SENIOR ROMAN OFFICERS HAD BEEN SACRIFICED ON BLOOD-DRENCHED PAGAN ALTARS (WE KNOW BECAUSE PARTS OF THEM WERE LEFT BEHIND).

At the end of Felix's chilling tale there was a scared silence in the barrack room. Lepidus deliberately swung the oil lamp hanging from the ceiling to make the shadows flicker and stretch around the walls. Then Felix blew out the lamplight and said:

"Sleep tight, boys," in a spooky voice!

MARCH 22ND AD59

This afternoon we polished our armour.
It was a boring job but, as Marius said, at least life in the army is better than some dead-end job back home. Felix said he joined to see the world and wear a uniform. Galerius joined for the good grub and Petrus said: "The pay's not bad and when I get to be top dog centurion it'll be even better."

"You joined to win the world for Rome!" barked Sejanus, who had crept up the corridor and was listening outside. "Now get some rest. We march for Britain tomorrow."

I hope this island isn't going to be as bad as it sounds, some kind of foggy bog full of pagan Celts. I wish I'd been sent somewhere warm, like Africa or Spain.

ME IN UNIFORM

LINEN UNDERSHIRT (HARD TO KEEP IT CLEAN ON THE MARCH) →

GALAE (MY TRUSTY HELMET)

LORICA SEGMENTATA (ARMOUR MADE OF METAL STRIPS)

WOOL TUNIC (ITCHY WHEN HOT)

GLADIUS – MY SWORD

PILUM – MY JAVELIN

CINGULUM (MY WAISTBAND – IT JINGLES WHEN I WALK. YOU KNOW THE LEGIONS ARE COMING WHEN YOU HEAR LOTS OF JINGLING!)

PUGIO – MY DAGGER

SCUTUM – (MY SHIELD, WITH A HARD POINTED BOSS FOR HITTING THE ENEMY)

CALIGAE – (MY HOBNAILED SANDALS, GOOD FOR MILES OF MARCHING)

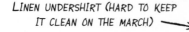

WATCH OUT CELTS, HERE I COME!

APRIL 3RD AD59
MARCHING ACROSS GAUL TO BRITAIN

Twenty miles' marching today, in the usual five
hours. We've practised it often enough, carrying
great loads of kit around the countryside until
we're all as strong as Hercules. Still, it would be
tough for an untrained soldier to carry all his
weapons and armour plus a poleful of tools,
rations, cooking equipment and all the rest.

He'd never make it out of the fort gate, let
alone to Britain.

Our tent and some of our stuff is being
carried by a mule. It's called Pallo and it's as
bad-tempered as a centurion with a sore head.
Just our luck.

Lucius has made up a little marching song to
pass the time and says it's so good I should
write it down, so here it is:

> "WE'RE IN THE BEST ARMY.
> WE'RE IN THE BEST LEGION.
> WE'RE IN THE BEST COHORT.
> WE'RE IN THE BEST CENTURY
> AND NOW YOU COME TO MENTION IT...
> THE BEST CONTURBENIUM!"

He might be in the best conturbenium but he's the worst singer I've ever heard.

APRIL 4TH AD59
ON THE WAY THROUGH GAUL

When we camped last night I felt so hungry I could have eaten a horse. Pallo must have read my mind because he tried to kick me as I unloaded the tent from his back. We made do with the usual marching rations - hard biscuits, cheese and a bit of bacon. "What will that mule eat?" asked Gaius. "The tent, probably," said Lepidus, then relented and gave him some oats.

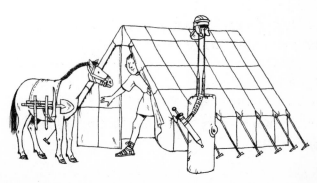

Centurion Sejanus came over and told us that because it was going to be cold in Britain we had permission to wear socks and underwear.

Felix said that only softies wore underwear and he would never be caught doing it. Gaius said that Felix would soon change his mind when the wind blew round his bum, and Gaius's mum had just sent him some spare socks and underwear that Felix could borrow. Felix swore he'd paint himself blue like a crack-brained Celt before he ever did that!

The lads are good fun to be with, which is just as well because I'll be stuck with them for a long time to come. Marius moans a lot and Lucius snores like a pig, but when it comes to battle we'll be standing side by side fighting for our lives, so we need to be friends. Sejanus will be with us too, though he's worse than an enemy because when he bullies us we can't fight back. He says we're all as lazy and useless as three-legged camels in a chariot race, and he uses more swear words about us than I ever knew existed in the Latin language.

◄━━▥▥━∘○∘━▤▤━►

APRIL 7TH AD59
STILL ON THE MARCH

I think my woollen tunic has got lice. I haven't got time to wash it so they'll have to come with me to Britain. I hope they like sailing. Personally, I'm terrified.

This morning we woke up earlier than the soldiers in the tent next door and found Pallo nibbling the kit they'd stacked outside. I hope they won't notice the spit on their shields!

We were sent out of the camp to catch some hares for the tribunes' dinner tonight. We set a trap on the edge of some dark, shadowy-looking woods and Lepidus decided to try to scare Gaius again. He started whispering, "I wouldn't be surprised if there were fierce wild boar hereabouts, you know, the ones with flesh-ripping tusks... not to mention ghosts with bony fingers for poking your eyes out..."

When we looked around Gaius had disappeared. The leaves rustled as if they were hissing at us. There was a weird drip, drip, drip sound. The shadows seemed to grow long and spiky... and Lepidus got very upset. He cried out that the ghosts had got Gaius and it was all his fault.

Suddenly Gaius jumped out from behind a tree trunk and shouted loudly. We almost jumped out of our armour and he doubled up laughing.

Good for Gaius. He may look like a kid straight from home but he's tough. He's not nearly as easy to scare as we thought.

April 10th ad59

My boat trip to Britain *has* to be the worst experience of my life so far. Petrus said it would only take a couple of hours to get across the water, which looked a sludgy grey colour. Those couple of hours felt like a very, very long time.

The boat was long, wooden and too low in the water for my liking. Pallo had the right idea and refused to go on board until Sejanus gave him a mighty thwack with his stick. Felix made things worse.

"I heard there are sea monsters in these parts," he said. I wasn't sure if he was teasing or not, but after that every big wave looked to me like the coil of some hungry giant sea serpent.

The boat had rowers on either side below deck (what an awful job). They seemed to know what they were doing, thank goodness. We soldiers stood crowded on deck with all our kit, getting spattered by sea spray. I soon felt miserably sick.

***

"You look as white as a ghost, Marcus," said Lucius. In fact I felt as if I'd died and gone down to Hades. I nearly threw up in my helmet but Sejanus looked me in the eye and said:

"Don't you dare, boy. If you mess up your equipment I'll have you digging ditches for weeks once we get to Britain."

In the end I did it over the side of the boat.

Luckily the wind didn't blow it back on to the rowers, or I might have been thrown over the side. I wasn't the only one to feel ill. Even Sejanus was looking a bit pale by the time we spied land.

"So this is Britain," Lucius said, and we all went quiet as a rocky ragged coastline loomed up ahead in the mist. What would we find there? Screaming savages on the shore? Ghost-ridden marshes where our tents would sink overnight without trace?

In fact when we finally arrived on shore we couldn't see anything at all in the freezing fog. "Welcome to Britain, boys," cried a Roman voice. "Hope you're wrapped up warm." Felix sidled up to Gaius and asked if he could borrow that spare underwear after all...

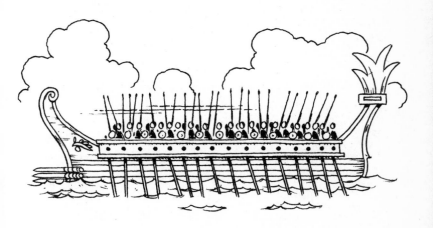

AUGUST 20TH AD59
ARMY FORTRESS AT DEVA, BRITAIN

I wonder if anyone in the future will read my
diary... If they do they'll probably be wondering
what happened to me in May, June and July.
The answer is, I've been kept so busy in the
fortress I've been too tired to write in the
evenings. Most of the legion is here and there's
a lot to do keeping everyone fed and healthy,
and preparing for the battles ahead. Every
morning we get our work orders and so far I've
been in the storehouses, the bakery, the hospital
rooms and the carpenter's shop, where they're
busy making flat-bottomed boats. We're going
to use them to make our first strike on the
enemy, an attack on the notorious Druid
hideout on the island of Mona.

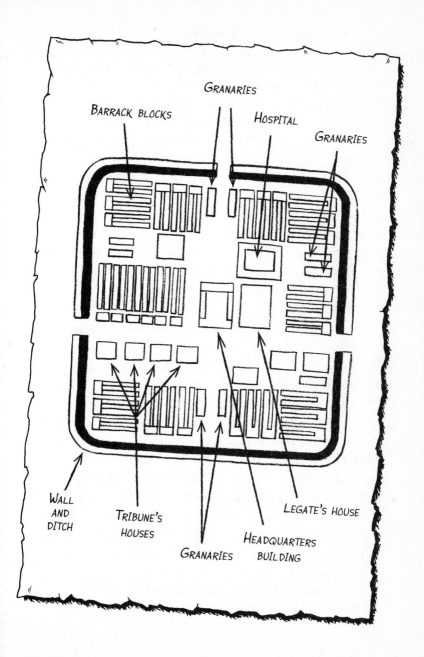

GRANARIES

BARRACK BLOCKS

HOSPITAL

GRANARIES

WALL
AND
DITCH

TRIBUNE'S
HOUSES

GRANARIES

HEADQUARTERS
BUILDING

LEGATE'S HOUSE

OCTOBER 8TH AD59

I was sitting on the toilet this morning, chatting away to some of the other lads in the toilet block. We've heard that the Celts are really getting angry with the Romans and apparently it's all the Druids' fault. They're a bunch of hardened Roman-haters and they've been stirring up trouble among the Celtic tribes from their base on Mona. We'll be sailing upriver to sort them out as soon as the weather gets better in spring. Apparently their leaders are high priests who perform some weird worship in sacred groves of oak trees on this island of theirs. They want to keep to their old ways and stay in charge, so we're not welcome.

Felix said you'd have thought the Celts would love Roman roads, riches, olive oil, baths, et cetera. "And underwear!" added Gaius. Felix nearly threw the bottom-cleaning sponge at him.

From what I hear, some of the Celtic tribes have been complaining about Roman behaviour generally. For instance, veteran Roman soldiers have set up a town at Camulodunum and the locals say they've been a bit rough, claiming farmland and executing people who make a fuss.

Some of the British tribes are friendly with us, of course. Just as well. Otherwise we'd have been sent packing long ago with long Celtic swords in our backs.

I'm sure that by the time someone in the future reads this diary the whole world will be

Roman. At the fort we're taking no chances though. There's a special decorated plaque fixed on the front gate to ward off evil. After all, the Celts are bound to use magic spells and curses against us. There's been lots of sacrificing and praying to our gods and goddesses to make sure that we win.

OCTOBER 11TH AD59

In Rome they'll be tasting the new wine today. There are loads of parties and feast days like that back home, and we're missing them all. Perhaps we could get the local Celts to celebrate some of them, though apparently they have a few special days of their own. Their party to celebrate the new year, called Samhain, is coming up at the end of this month. They light bonfires and try to keep away the evil spirits that come along at this time of year. Then they jump over the bonfires and play tricks on each other. It sounds like a wild party and I'd quite like to join in, though I don't like the sound of the evil spirits much.

NOVEMBER 16TH AD59

I keep losing to Lucius whenever we play a dice game. He says he's got lucky because last week he made an offering to the gods, a little statue or something. I ought to give that a try.

Gaius has got a lucky ring with a picture of the goddess Diana on it, and he says I can borrow it if I let him write in my diary.

So I've left a little space for him below.

GAIUS IS
BRILLIANT!
SEJANUS
IS A
TOILET
SPONGE

NOVEMBER 17TH AD59

I was on guard at the fortress headquarters today and I saw Suetonius Paullinus, the Roman governer of the whole country. He was in a meeting with all the main legion officers.
I wonder what it was all about. Does it mean we'll be fighting soon?

Afterwards we were told to sweep the floor by a stuck-up military tribune who probably only got the job because his father's a senator. His nose was so long he reminded me of Pallo the mule, and he looked down at us as if we were a bad smell from the Imperial sewers. If he ever gets his head copied in marble they'll need extra stone for a snout like that. Petrus says all top Romans have "distinctive facial extremities". That's big noses to you and me. Petrus has got one.

DECEMBER 17TH AD59

It's the start of Saturnalia, twelve days of partying back in Rome. All sorts of things go on back home, some of them too rude to write about! The best bit of Saturnalia is getting lots of gifts. I remember getting a bag of sweets and a toy sword when I was a kid. Thinking about it makes me feel homesick, and I know the others are feeling the same way. I moan about the weather, Galerius moans about the food and Marius moans about everything.

DECEMBER 29TH AD59

We were all out on the fortress parade ground today, every rank, from the legate down to the legionaries. The signifiers looked really smart in their bearskins. I'd like to reach that rank one day so I could carry the century's standard and pay out the soldiers' wages from a big coin-filled chest. The bearskin would be handy in cold weather too. If I'm good enough I might even get promoted to the rank of centurion eventually. Then I'll be able to boss everyone around.

DECEMBER 30TH AD59

I got paid my wages in denarii coins by our signifier. His name is Camillus and he always looks grumpy, as if someone in hobnailed army sandals is standing on his toes. But he's good at maths so we trust him with our pay.
I wish I'd worked a bit harder at maths when I went to school back home. My mother used to send me along to the class at the end of the street and we used to sit outside under an awning struggling with our work. I was very easily distracted by the things going on in the street – people shopping, collecting water from the well, dogs fighting, babies crying. My teacher said I'd end up as 'some good-for-nothing street pickpocket' if I didn't work harder.

MY LEGION

LEGATE – THE BIG CHEESE IN CHARGE, FROM A TOP ROMAN FAMILY →

TRIBUNES – SIX SNOOTY STAFF OFFICERS, USUALLY FROM TOP FAMILIES ↘

PRAEFECTUS CASTRORUM – CAMP PREFECT, THE HIGHEST US ORDINARY SOLDIERS CAN GO →

ONE DAY THIS WILL BE MARCUS GALLO!

PRIMUS PILUS – TOP BULLY CENTURION ↙

CENTURIONS – THE REST OF THE BULLIES ↘

OPTIOS – CENTURIONS – IN–WAITING (LEARNING TO BE BULLIES!) ↙

SIGNIFIERS – IN CHARGE OF THE PAY AND THE STANDARDS. THEY'RE THE ONES WITH BEARSKINS ON THEIR BACKS.

LEGIONARIES – ORDINARY SOLDIERS LIKE ME

TESSERARI – GUARD COMMANDERS

JANUARY 3RD AD60
BARRACK ROOM AT THE FORTRESS

I've just loosened my belt because I feel as full
as an Emperor's treasure chest. Why? Because it
was Galerius's turn to cook for our barrack
room today and he made an extra-special effort
to cheer us up. He barbecued chicken on the
cooking grate outside and ground up herbs,
spices and oil to make his own top-secret sauce
for it. At the end he added olives from one of
the jars brought from Rome, and they really
reminded us all of home. Galerius said that if
we're going to fight soon, we should do it with
some good food in our bellies, and if we win
he'll cook us a feast fit for an emperor. He's
even made up an imaginary menu for our
victory banquet, and he told me to write it
down.

DREAM DINNER

COOKED BY GALERIUS, THE GREAT ROMAN CHEF

(HE TOLD ME TO WRITE THAT BIT).

REMOVAL OF GUESTS' SHOES
(SANDALS WILL BE PROVIDED BY THE HOST).
PRAYER TO JUPITER AND TO THE HOUSEHOLD GODS.

FIRST COURSE

MILK–FED SNAILS
STUFFED DORMICE
OSTRICH BRAINS

MAIN COURSE

ROASTED VENISON WITH DATE SAUCE
ROAST BARNACLE GOOSE
PEACOCK RISSOLES STEWED IN HONEY
AND PEPPER
PEAS MIXED WITH GRAINS OF GOLD

OFFERINGS MADE TO THE HOUSEHOLD GODS
(EG: FOOD THROWN INTO THE FIRE)

DESSERT

STUFFED DATES
HONEY CAKES
WATERED–DOWN WINE SWEETENED WITH
HONEY AND ROSE PETALS

ENTERTAINMENT: DANCING GIRLS AND JUGGLERS.

SLAVES TO CARRY GUESTS AWAY AT MIDNIGHT.

Galerius's top Roman cooking has made us forget our moans and groans, and we've been telling each other funny stories about our lives. Felix has a really good one which he says I can write down.

HE WAS WALKING PAST THE CHARIOT RACING STADIUM IN ROME ONE DAY, AVOIDING THE DODGY SOUVENIR SELLERS, THE SMELLY TAKEAWAY STALLS AND THE FAKE ASTROLOGERS WAITING TO TELL YOU LIES FOR YOUR MONEY. SUDDENLY AN OLD TOOTHLESS WOMAN GRABBED HIM BY THE ARM.

"IT'S YOUR LUCKY DAY," SHE CACKLED. "THE GODS ARE SMILING ON YOU! I KNOW. I CAN SEE THE FUTURE."

WELL, FELIX HADN'T MEANT TO GO TO THE RACES BECAUSE HE DIDN'T HAVE MUCH MONEY, BUT AFTER THE ASTROLOGER'S PREDICTION HE DECIDED HE MIGHT AS WELL TRY IT. HIS SPORTING HERO AT THAT TIME WAS A CHARIOTEER CALLED ANTONIUS, A SUPERSTAR PIN-UP WITH HIS PICTURE ALL OVER ROME, WHO'D WON MORE MONEY AND RICHES THAN YOU COULD FIT IN A ROMAN BATH. ANTONIUS WAS LUCKY BECAUSE HE'D LIVED TO THE RIPE OLD AGE OF TWENTY-FIVE, AND MOST CHARIOTEERS HAVE BEEN CRUSHED OR TRAMPLED ON THE RACETRACK BY THAT AGE.

FELIX FELT LUCKY, TOO, AFTER THE ASTROLOGER'S PROMISE. HE BET ALL HIS MONEY ON ANTONIUS.

CIRCUS MAXIMUS – ROME

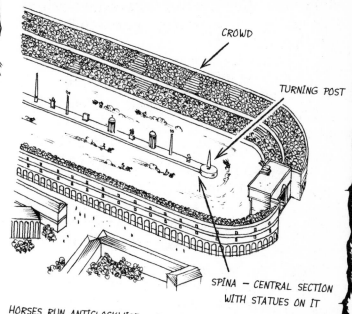

CROWD

TURNING POST

SPINA – CENTRAL SECTION
WITH STATUES ON IT

HORSES RUN ANTICLOCKWISE – BUMPING AND RAMMING ALLOWED!!

THE EMPEROR NERO WAS THERE THAT AFTERNOON. HE LOVES SPORT SO HE'S ALWAYS ORGANISING GAMES AND SHOWS. WHEN HE SIGNALLED, THE TRUMPET BLEW AND THE FIRST RACE BEGAN. THE CROWD WENT WILD AS THE CHARIOTS THUNDERED OUT OF THEIR STALLS AND SPED OFF ROUND THE TRACK. AS USUAL A COUPLE OF THEM CRASHED AND THEIR DRIVERS FELL OFF. BUT ANTONIUS WAS GOING WELL, AND FELIX WAS CHEERING HIM ON AS HE WAS CONTROLLING HIS HORSE EXPERTLY USING THE REINS WRAPPED ROUND HIS WAIST.

He was comfortably in front until he made a mistake, let his horses brush up against the wall in the middle of the track, and one of the religious statues fell down from the top!

He carried on but the crowd went quiet because they were scared that the gods would be offended. They were looking anxiously up into the sky for thunderbolts.

Felix felt scared, too, though not because of heavenly lightning. He thought he'd lost the last of his money!

The gods were angry and showed it because a wheel fell off Antonius's chariot (either that or someone had sabotaged it). He quickly cut the reins with his knife and jumped clear but his horses ran wild, crashed into the chariot behind and there was a huge pile-up.

In the end nobody reached the finishing line and the crowd were really angry. Felix said it was pretty frightening and they might have rioted if Nero hadn't taken charge. He had free gifts and lottery tickets thrown at them to make them feel happy again. Felix caught a lottery ticket and that's how he won his money back, plus quite a lot more.

The astrologer had been right all along!

Felix's story made us laugh
and reminded us all of some
of the good times we've
had back home.
I wonder what that old
astrologer would say about
our chances of ever
making it back there...

JANUARY 4TH AD60

I'm going to make a list of all the things
I miss from home (and the things I don't, to
remind myself that it's not all perfect!).

THINGS I MISS FROM HOME
THE CHARIOT RACES,
ESPECIALLY SEEING MY TEAM, THE BLUES,
BEATING THE REDS, GREENS AND WHITES!

UP THE BLUES!

FRESH DATES
WARM SUNSHINE
THE SHOPS THAT LINE THE STREETS OF ROME
THE GOSSIP
(WHAT WILL THE EMPEROR'S FAMILY
GET UP TO NEXT?)

MY MOTHER, FATHER, BROTHER AND SISTER –
I MUST GET A LETTER TO THEM SOON.

THINGS I DEFINITELY DON'T MISS FROM HOME

THE SMELL IN THE ROMAN STREETS WHEN IT'S HOT
(ESPECIALLY NEAR THE FISH MARKET)
THE CROWDS IN THE FORUM
HORRIBLE TAKEAWAYS
(ESPECIALLY CALF'S HEAD IN COLD GRAVY)
PICKPOCKETS
THE RED, GREEN AND WHITE CHARIOT TEAMS –
WHAT A LOAD OF RUBBISH!

Maybe Britain will turn out to have some good things about it, after all.

Here's hoping.

FEBRUARY 24TH AD60
AT THE FORTRESS

Yesterday was our Roman Festival of Terminalia to celebrate the end of the old year. We went for a drink in the tavern last night, in the Vicus settlement along the outside wall of the fort. The Celts who live there are the ones who work for the fort so they're not our enemies. At least they weren't until Lucius and I started singing our new marching song in the street and we started all the local dogs off barking!

Everyone knows February is an unlucky month. That must be the reason why I've got a headache today.

March 1st ad60

I was sent out to a friendly Celtic village today to get some animal skins and beer for the fort. The village was just a few round huts with dogs and chickens running around. While I was waiting for the supplies, the sun shone so warmly I took off my cloak. A pretty girl with dark hair and green eyes smiled at me and offered me some honey cakes from a basket. Her little brother came up to me shyly and touched my armour. These people didn't seem strange or fierce. They've been friendly with the Romans for nearly twenty years now so they speak a little Latin, and standing there happily in the sunshine, munching cake, I felt quite at home. It's a shame not all Celts give us such a warm welcome.

March 2nd ad60
Back at the fortress

My cloak is missing! I'm sure someone has stolen
it. Last night I went to wrap it round my head in
bed and it wasn't there, so I had to listen to the
snoring again and now I'm tired and bad-tempered.
I can't go marching off to fight without a cloak
and it'll cost me a fortune to buy a new one.
I'll have to ask Camillus the signifier to take it
out of my savings. What a bad start to the
Roman New Year.

REMINDER:

GET A CURSE WRITTEN ON A PIECE OF LEAD
AND DROP IT DOWN THE BATH DRAIN SO THE
UNDERWORLD GODS GET THE MESSAGE.

TO PLVTO GOD OF THE VNDERWORLD
PLEASE CVRSE THE PERSON WHO
STOLE MY CLOAK MAY THEIR TEETH
FALL OVT ONE BY ONE THIS CVRSE WAS
WRITTEN BY MARCVS GALLO

MARCH 3RD AD60

I am still angry about my cloak but it was our turn at the baths today and that made me feel a bit better. I won at all the ball games we played (until Felix accidentally burst the pig's bladder we were using for a ball). Then we covered ourselves with olive oil and got our skin scraped by the servants. Marius had his chest and toe hairs plucked out. He moaned all the time about the pain, but at least he looks civilised again. You won't catch a decent Roman with any body hair.

ME SIZZLING IN THE HOT CALDARIUM

STRIGIL (SCRAPER)

OIL

ME RELAXING IN THE WARM TEPIDARIUM

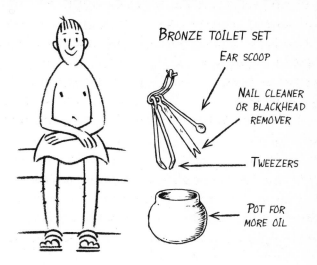

BRONZE TOILET SET

EAR SCOOP

NAIL CLEANER
OR BLACKHEAD
REMOVER

TWEEZERS

POT FOR
MORE OIL

ME PLUNGING INTO A COLD BATH
IN THE FRIGIDARIUM!

DISH TO SPLASH
COLD WATER
OVER MYSELF

FANTASTIC!

Later on I dropped my curse down the drain when I thought no one was looking, but Lepidus saw me and asked what I was doing.

I admitted that I'd lost my cloak and the other boys said it was sure to have been stolen by the thieving Celts in the village I visited. I was stupid to think they were friendly and I'm going to report them.

They'll be in big trouble when I've finished with them.

Just as we were coming out of the baths we heard an awful shout from the hospital block. The camp doctor was pulling out someone's rotten tooth with pliers, and they must have needed quite a few people to hold the patient down by the sound of it.

MARCH 5TH AD60

We found out that the dentist's patient was our very own Centurion Sejanus! At first we laughed about it, but we soon went quiet when we found out that he was giving us extra training. He was in a terrible temper because he had a sore mouth, and he probably had a hangover too. Apparently the doctor got him drunk so he wouldn't feel the pain so much.

As a result our extra training meant extra bullying and shouting. Bring on the Druids! They can't be as bad as him!

MARCH 6TH AD60

Because we'll be marching soon the legion's commanders thought we should have a treat, so today there was a show in the fortress's amphitheatre. The legion can't afford lions and star gladiators so we saw a wild boar being chased and killed, some wrestling and a local prisoner being executed.

I'd like to have seen a British bear fighting the boar but Petrus says when they catch bears they ship them to Rome for the big exciting shows. The prisoner who got executed was a thief. If I report the Celts in the village for stealing my cloak I suppose they might get executed too. But what if they didn't do it? I need to be sure. I'll go back and take a look at that girl's teeth.

If my curse is working on her I'll know she's guilty.

MARCH 7TH AD60

Our spies have been out and about in the eastern part of the country and they say there could be serious trouble brewing. Apparently there's a tribe in the east of the country called the Iceni. Their king has died and our Roman officials have moved in to claim their kingdom. The widow, Queen Boudicca, has been flogged and her daughters were attacked. Her people are very angry and they're going to fight back.

MARCH 8TH AD60

I went back to the Celtic village and the girl
with the green eyes was there. "I lost my cloak.
I thought it might be here," I told her, using
simple Latin and a lot of pointing and hand
signals. As I explained my problem I tried to
think of a way of getting a look at her teeth.
I was about to lose my temper and start accusing
her of stealing, but just in time she smiled at me
and I saw that her teeth were beautiful, just like
the rest of her.

She replied with her own hand signals and a
little Latin along the lines of: "Last time you
came I think you put it in one of your
saddlebags."

I looked inside Pallo's saddlebag and, sure
enough, my cloak was stuffed right down in the
bottom. Thank the gods I didn't accuse her of
stealing. She told me her name was Ena; then she
took me for a walk around the fields and told me
that she helps her family grow and harvest crops.
That sort of life's all right if the weather is good
enough for the crops to grow, but if the harvest
failed they'd all starve. I suppose we'd help them
out with some of our grain stores. Aren't they
lucky we're around!

Ena and I understood each other pretty well.
I don't know a single Celtic word, but she knows
enough of my language for us to communicate.

She invited me into her father's hut, which was clean but very smoky because there's a fire but no chimney. Then she asked what houses were like in Rome and I told her about the grand ones with wall paintings, private gardens and lots of slaves. I really boasted about Rome but she saw through me and said: "What about the poor people?" I had to admit that some Romans have to rent tiny damp rooms in rotting blocks of flats that might tumble down at any minute.

When it was time to leave Pallo wasn't outside the hut and I panicked for a moment, thinking he'd been stolen too. Then I saw him eating the thatched roof of someone's hut. Ena stroked him and put a flower behind his ear. He ate it on the way home.

March 10th ad60

Today I was called to one of the fortress gates.

"There's someone to see you. He says it's very important," said one of the sentries, and winked.

When I looked outside I couldn't see anyone. Then I looked down and there was Ena's brother, the little boy from the Celtic village. He only came up to my knees.

"Ena sent this for you," he said, pressing a small package into my hands. "She says you're to take it with you when you go off to fight. It'll bring you luck."

The boy scampered off leaving me with the sentries.

"Present from your girlfriend?" they giggled. "Let's see!" One of them grabbed the mystery gift and unwrapped the cloth. Inside there was a small metal brooch shaped like a running hare.

"A Celtic good luck charm," he smiled, giving it back to me. "I hope it works, mate."

I hid behind the bakery and pinned the brooch to my tunic, on the inside where no one would see it. How strange that I should be wearing a Celtic charm to fight the rebel Celts…

June 3rd ad60
Marching through Wales

Finally we're on the move, marching towards a river where we'll launch our boats for the Druid hideout on the island of Mona. There are no camps or fortresses on the way so we're building temporary camps every time we stop for the night. Half of us go on guard while the other half dig ditches, pile up earth and stick in the stakes that will keep our enemies out.

We legionaries are very good at digging. If you need a defensive ditch or a nice big earth rampart we're the men for you. Or perhaps you'd like a lily trap, a great big camouflaged hole in the ground with sharp stakes at the bottom. If your enemy happens to come along, whoosh! He falls in the hole and ends up stuck on a stick.

In between digging camps we march along but Wales isn't a friendly place and the atmosphere is quite forbidding. There are no cheery waves from children as we go past; in fact we don't see anyone. Petrus says there are probably spies watching us from hiding places, then running off to tell the Druids we're coming.

We stack our weapons carefully outside our tent so we can get at them quickly if we're ambushed.

June 10th ad60

We reached the Isle of Mona in our boats, and the shoreline was a weird sight. Priestesses in long robes and wild bushy hair waved flaming torches and screamed at us. The Druid high priests held their hands up and called down awful curses. For a few seconds we all felt terrified. After all, these fanatics are supposed to sacrifice their prisoners on blood-covered altars or burn them alive in cages. They decorate their homes with the heads of their enemies, like sculpture. I've heard they sometimes put an enemy head on the table at mealtimes.

Shocked by the sight, we hesitated until one of our generals shouted out.

"Romans! You are the very best! Do not fear the enemy!" We jumped out of the boats with a great cry.

COME ON
ROMANS!
ATTACK!

June 12th AD60
On the way back to Deva

When I think about the fighting on Mona it is just a blur. Once my feet touched the shore it was as if I forgot who I was. My training took over and I concentrated completely on my weapons. Terrible fighting raged around me yet I was able to block it out and I could only hear the sound of the centurions shouting orders. I was aware of Lucius and Gaius standing on either side of me as we surged forward, cutting down the enemy with our swords.

When it was over, and the Druid base was destroyed, I looked down and realised I was spattered with blood. It was as if I had woken from a dream; I suddenly felt sick and staggered blindly. An older legionary steadied me and patted me on the back.

"Your first time is hard, son. They don't teach you about feelings in training, do they? Well, fighting is your job and you did it well. Now you must let the memory go. Block the details from your mind and concentrate on getting yourself cleaned up and having a decent night's sleep."

Funnily enough everyone else must have felt the same. Nobody talked about the fighting in our tent. We were all very quiet, lost in our own thoughts.

JUNE 13TH AD60

Although we have destroyed the rebel Druids,
which should have been a great victory, we have
been told some terrible news. Across to the east
the Iceni have attacked the Roman town of
Camulodunum and killed everyone. A survivor
brought the awful news. When the Celts attacked
there were no legions there to fight back – just
old soldiers, women and children. They held out
for as long as they could in the town temple,
hoping for a rescue that never came.

Apparently before it happened there were
lots of warning signs from the gods, so people
had some idea that there was going to be a
disaster. A statue of the goddess Victoria fell
over for no reason and there were ghostly
howling noises in the town. The sea turned the
colour of blood and phantom bodies were
washed up on the shore. Petrus says this is all
rubbish, stories that were probably spread about
by enemy Celtic spies to scare the Roman-
supporting townspeople. Scared or not, they
fought bravely to the end and we must
avenge them.

JUNE 20TH AD60

As we hurried back to Deva we got more awful
news from our spies. Soldiers of the Ninth Legion
have been killed in an enemy Celtic ambush as

they marched towards Camulodunum. Their legate narrowly escaped with his life by battling through the enemy ranks and then riding like the wind back to his base. My guess is that the Ninth got ambushed in the woods, Varus-style, perhaps when they were spread out in a long marching line. The rebel Celts must have been watching them from the trees, waiting for just the right time to attack. What a cruel and cowardly tactic.

JUNE 25TH AD60
BACK AT THE FORTRESS

News has come from Rome that the Emperor Nero's mother is dead. I hope it isn't a bad omen.

(At this point in his diary Marcus has written in code because if he was found writing anything bad about the Emperor he'd probably be executed in some horrible way.)

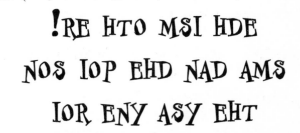

!RE HTO MSI HDE

NOS IOP EHD NAD AMS

IOR ENY ASY EHT

Can you crack the code? The answer's on page 95.

June 28th AD60
Still at the fortress

Sejanus told us to check that all our weapons and kit were in good shape because we could be going into action again at any time.
To take our minds off it all we played dice before going to bed, and Lucius tried to cheer us all up with a joke.

IF A GREEK, A ROMAN AND A CELT WERE LEFT ON AN ISLAND THE GREEK WOULD START A POEM, THE ROMAN WOULD START A ROAD AND THE CELT WOULD START A FIGHT.

Unfortunately, they've started the fight with *us*.

July 5th AD60
On the march from Deva down Watling Street towards Londinium

Suetonius Paullinus has taken some of our fastest cavalry and ridden off towards the town of Londinium to see what's going on. He thinks the rebel Celts will attack there next.

We're following on foot, except for the auxiliary soldiers on horseback. The auxiliaries are a funny bunch. They're not from Rome, of course, so they don't have Roman citizenship. They speak in foreign accents and come mostly from Roman outposts such as Thrace or Dacia. When they retire they'll become Roman citizens, so it's worth their while to join up. They do us a favour by fighting and we give them membership of the most powerful club on earth – the Roman Empire. This lot of auxiliaries have run out of luck and they've been sent to Britain to drown in the rain with us.

At night we camp and go over our battle tactics again, reminding ourselves of the battle formations we've learnt. We're very organised and when we meet the rebel Celts we'll be ready for them. We'll be a line of impenetrable Roman shields marching forwards to mow them down.

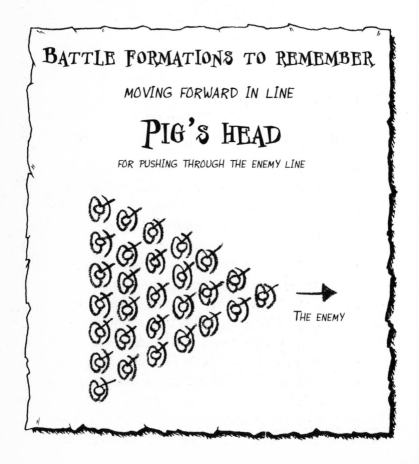

BATTLE FORMATIONS TO REMEMBER

MOVING FORWARD IN LINE

PIG'S HEAD

FOR PUSHING THROUGH THE ENEMY LINE

THE ENEMY

SQUARE

USE IF WE GET SURROUNDED BY THE ENEMY

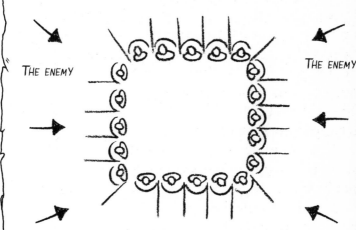

THE ENEMY

THE ENEMY

THE ENEMY

TORTOISE

WE WON'T NEED THIS BUT I LIKE PRACTISING IT!
USE TO GET CLOSE TO AN ENEMY BUILDING UNDER SIEGE

THE ENEMY

July 12th AD60

Suetonius Paullinus has returned from Londinium, riding hard with an escort of horsemen. He could see that it was hopeless to try to defend it from the enemy Celts, who are on their way to destroy it. The townspeople are fleeing down the river in any boats they can find, or struggling up Watling Street to safety behind our lines. Anyone who doesn't make it out of the city will probably die and there's nothing we can do to stop it happening.

Once they've destroyed Londinium the Celts will probably turn our way and our army may not be big enough to defeat them. We could do with some more men, so the governor has ordered the Second Augusta Legion up from Isca to join us. They should be arriving any day now.

July 18th AD60

The Second Augusta soldiers still haven't joined us. Surely they should be here by now? I hope they haven't been ambushed on the way. We're running out of time so they need to hurry up. Soon the enemy Celts will be swarming up Watling Street from Londinium, with the sole purpose of wiping us out. Petrus says they'll probably stop to destroy the town of Verulamium on the way, though the townspeople have had time to escape by now. If the enemy delay for a little while, that'll give us a few extra days to find a good battleground, but on the other hand we need to fight pretty soon because we're running short of food supplies. A few hard biscuits and some watery porridge won't keep us going for much longer.

The countryside is very empty and wild, with just a few poor Celtic villages here and there. The villagers hide when we march by. I get the impression they think we're doomed.

WHERE IS THE SECOND AUGUSTA LEGION?

WE NEED THEM!

TRUMPETERS (CORNICENS)

LEGIONARIES

THE **XX** VALERIA LEGION MARCHING IN A LONG LINE TOWARDS BATTLE

SIGNIFIERS
CARRYING STANDARDS

AQUILA
THE MOST IMPORTANT STANDARD

AUXILIARY CAVALRY

July 21st AD60
Camping on the march down
Watling Street

I can't help thinking of Ena. Has she put a love spell on me? How can I be thinking about a Celtic girl when I'm about to go into battle and kill a lot of her people?

The answer, I suppose, is that I've come to see that Celts aren't all the same. Some are murderous fighters who hate us, and some are our allies, beginning to live in the Roman way. Ena and her family are amongst our allies, but if we lose against the rebels who knows what will happen to them. I pray to the gods that I get the chance to see her again.

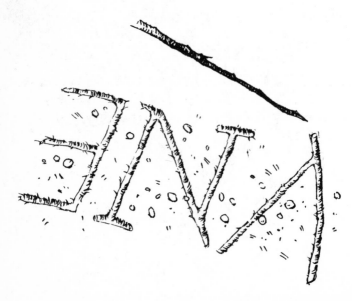

JULY 22ND AD60
CAMPING ON THE MARCH

Disaster! Lepidus saw me writing Ena's name in the dirt outside the tent. Now everyone is teasing me.

"Hey, Marcus. Are we all invited to your Celtic wedding?" jeered Gaius.

"Oi, Marcus. You thought she stole your cloak, but she stole your heart."

On and on they went, until I got sick of the teasing, wrapped my cloak around my head and went off to sleep early in the tent.

Things went from bad to worse.

I thought I was dreaming when I heard a high voice calling me:

> "Marcus, Marcus. It's me, Ena.
> Kiss your true love!"

Sleepily I puckered up my lips for a dream kiss. I felt warm breath on my cheeks... only it stank of cabbage! I woke up to find the others laughing their heads off. Pallo had stuck his head through the tent door and was breathing in my face.

Despite their teasing I feel very close to my fellow soldiers. I hope we all survive to laugh together in our old age, sitting in some far-off Roman tavern, perhaps by the warm blue Mediterranean Sea. We'll remember our days as army men long, long ago, when we conquered Britain and had our most glorious battle.

Galerius will probably own the tavern by then. Felix and Lepidus will be running a school for gladiators. Lucius will be married to some rich Roman lady and Petrus will collect taxes. Marius will be moaning on a market stall and Gaius will probably be running the army. Me? Either I'll be the Emperor's right-hand man, or I'll still be a legionary on toilet-cleaning duties. It depends if I please the gods or not.

OH, MARS ULTOR,
GOD OF WAR,
LOOK AFTER ALL
YOUR LOYAL SERVANTS IN
THE BATTLE TO COME.
ESPECIALLY ME
AND MY MATES.

JULY 24TH AD60
A BATTLEFIELD IN THE MIDLANDS

We've stopped marching because our commanders have chosen a site that looks like it will make a good battleground for us. Now we're waiting for the Celts to arrive. Last night we heard Sejanus chatting with one of the other centurions, and we realised just how serious our position is.

"Either the Celts will wipe us out - no more Roman rule – or we'll crush them forever," he said. Either way the future of the country hangs in the balance.

We've been lucky that the enemy didn't arrive sooner, and we've been able to choose a good place to fight. We've got a wooded hill behind us, which will protect our rear. The enemy has to attack us from the front, though if we lose we'll be trapped (we mustn't lose!). In front of us there's a flat plain between two hills.

Towards us the plain gets narrower so the enemy will get crushed up together as they charge forwards at us. They carry very long swords, and by the time they reach us they won't have enough room to use them properly.

Tonight we won't put up tents. We'll catch sleep when we can, leaning on rolled-up cloaks and packs. The sky is very clear and there's a big moon, shining like a coin from our pay chest. The enemy Celts will like a big moon. They'll probably see it as a good omen.

I touch Ena's brooch. I feel the shape of the running hare, a magical creature of the moon. Can its Celtic charm work for me, a Roman?

Galerius has just come up to me and slipped something into my hand. It's a piece of honey cake! He says he's been saving some in his pack for an emergency, and now seems as good a time as any to hand it round.

We munch silently on it, watching lights flicker over the hills. The Celts are arriving.

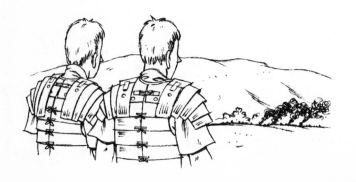

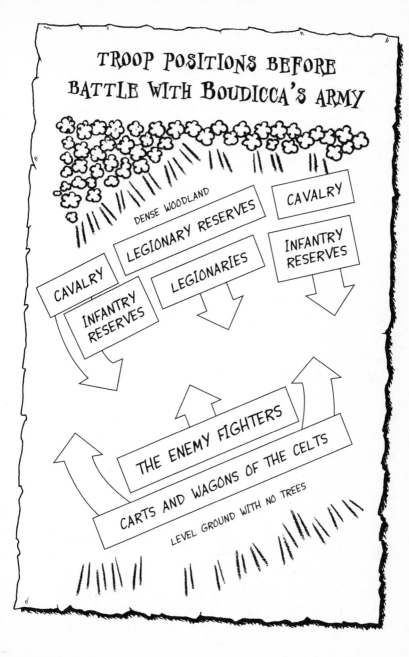

We've just had a report from the scouts. Gaius overheard them when he was wandering near the commanders' tent. Apparently there are hundreds and thousands of Celts arriving and we've only got 13,000 men! There's no sign of the Second Augusta Legion. It's clear they're not coming. Well, they'll be sorry they missed the fight when we all become heroes. We'll deserve every medal going if we beat this mighty rabble.

JULY 25TH AD60
EARLY MORNING BEFORE BATTLE

Sejanus has just sat us all down and talked to us about the battle. The legionaries will be put in the centre at the front of the battle line. The auxiliary foot soldiers will stand either side of us and the auxiliary cavalry units will be on the wings.

During the battle we must listen for commands relayed to us by horn signals, and at all costs we must protect our standards (that means rallying round our grumpy old signifier Camillus). If we lose a standard it will be a disgrace to the legion. We mustn't let that happen. Sejanus surprised us by giving us some praise.

He started by saying, "It'll be harder than Mona tomorrow. You'll be facing proper warriors this time. But you're all good lads, well-trained and brave. I know you'll be a credit to the legion. Fight well, remember what I've taught you and make sure you help your mates if they need you."

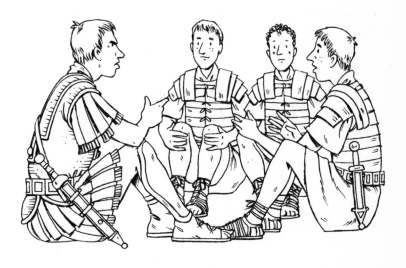

He started to walk away and then turned to say one last thing:

"I want to see you all back when it's over."

This could be the last entry I shall write in my diary. I shall leave it in Pallo's saddlebag, and hope we both survive the day.

July 30th ad60
After the battle with Boudicca's army

Before it all began I stood there with 13,000 other soldiers, my metal helmet shining in the sun for every one of the enemy to aim at, and a hard knot of fear growing in my stomach. I kept repeating to myself over and over again what the Emperor Julius Caesar had once said: *Only fear the first charge of the Celts*. He knew that the pagans would make one fierce charge but after that they would be a disorganised rabble. Well, that first charge was about to happen and I was pretty scared.

I looked across at Lucius and he winked at me but I could see he was pale beneath his helmet. We knew what to expect - the Celtic trumpets and horns would blow. The maddest bravest pagan warriors would charge towards us at the front of their army, naked except for magical symbols painted on their bodies. According to our spies there were as many as 100,000 other warriors behind these naked madmen, all of them desperate to crush the hated Roman invaders.

I knew we had the finest army in the world but what if the Celts did have magic on their side? Later on, of course, we found out they were so certain of winning they had brought their wives and children along to watch the battle. They sat on top of their wagons around the battlefield for a grandstand view.

While we stood, silent and still, we could hear the Celts shouting challenges and insults, working themselves into a frenzy. Every now and again one of their small chariots came out from their battle line towards us, pulled by a pair of wide-eyed snorting horses in a show-off display of fast driving. In each chariot there was a driver and a warrior with a deadly collection of spears.

THE CELTS SHOUT, SCREAM AND SHOW OFF IN FRONT OF US.

CELTIC LONG SWORD

CELTIC BATTLE CHARIOT

"Look, there's Queen Boudicca," whispered Lucius and sure enough, in the distance we could see a tall red-headed woman in a chariot riding to and fro in front of her troops, probably giving them some speech to make them feel brave.

Our leader, Suetonius Paullinus, rode out in front of our lines and gave us a rousing speech, too, to make us feel brave and proud to be fighting for Rome. Our Emperor wasn't with us in person of course, but we had his picture, the imago, fixed on a special battle standard, so he fought with us in spirit. We fought for the Roman Emperor; they fought for the wild woman with the red hair.

Paullinus rode away behind our lines. Then, just for a second, the air around me seemed to go very quiet and still. A bee buzzed past and it reminded me of the fruit orchards at home in summer. I thought to myself that I'd like to take Ena there one day...

Then my fleeting daydream was wiped out by the sound of war horns followed by a terrible roar that echoed around the hills.

A line of crazy Celts streamed towards me. In front of the charge Boudicca rode in her chariot with her two daughters. She looked terrifying, brave beyond belief, as her long red hair streamed out behind her.

"Hold your line," cried Sejanus. "Hold your line!" Stones from Celtic slingshots flew overhead. It seemed to me that we waited forever as that army charged towards us, pressed in ever more closely together by the slopes on either side of them...

Then at last our order came: a trumpet signal and a loud shout from our side that made me feel brave again. Thousands of flashing Roman javelins soared upwards into the sky and down towards the enemy. Then thousands more rained down on them and finally, with a great roar, we bowed our heads down behind our shields and surged towards the enemy.

We marched in a tight line towards them, pressing them backwards along the valley. I felt invincible as we stabbed and stabbed again, moving forward as if we were gods ourselves and nothing could stop us. They had no room to swing their great long swords at us. They had the wrong weapons, the wrong armour, the wrong tactics... brave but hopelessly old-fashioned fighters, a disorganised rabble up against an unstoppable line of advancing shields. If our line ever grew ragged horn signals drew us back to re-form and advance once more, and if a legionary fell, another took his place. As I conquered with my comrades I felt truly powerful, that I was a ruler of the world. Still, war is war and it's dangerous for every man. I fought for a long time, trying not to make the mistake that would cost me my life. It went on for hours, but when I think of it now it seems to me as if the battle took hardly any time at all. Perhaps time stood still that day to watch the new destroying the old.

After a while I got careless, perhaps because I could see we were winning. I felt something slash my arm; I slipped and dropped my shield. I seemed to fall slowly and silently and saw a Celt with spiked hair and a long sword above me. I could almost touch the magic symbols painted on his chest.

"Running hare, I need you now," I muttered. Then my enemy fell, stabbed from the side, and Sejanus, my very own bad-tempered old centurion, pulled me to my feet.

"Come on lad, grab another shield. You can't have a rest yet." He'd saved my life.

At the end our cavalry rode in from either side and killed what was left of the enemy; and anyone left on the wagons too. They'd come to watch the show but ended up taking part by losing their lives.

The Celts were utterly destroyed; I heard there were tens of thousands of enemy dead;

only about four hundred of our men were killed.

My own little group of weary soldiers had survived, each with our own battle tale to tell; each with our own scars that would always remind us of the day we fought side by side.

My arm was cut quite badly. One of our medical orderlies bandaged it up. He said I would be sent back to Deva where the army doctors would stitch the wound.

Sejanus came over to see the damage.

"You'll be all right, although you'll have a scar I should think," he said. I thanked him for saving my life.

"Training saved your life, lad," he said. "Stab low, stab low!" He winked and walked away.

To hide the tears in my eyes I dropped my head and saw something lying in the dust. I bent over, picked it up with my good arm, and rubbed the dirt off with my finger. It was an Iceni coin with a picture of a horse on it. I'll keep it to remember the day I helped conquer a country for the Empire.

SEPTEMBER 1ST AD60
ARMY FORTRESS AT DEVA

An army doctor has cleaned my wound with turpentine and stitched it up. The herbal healing medicine he's given me is disgusting. Some of the wounded men had limbs amputated, so I was lucky and shouldn't complain.

I suppose I ought to spend my days helping around the place as best I can but it's a bit lonely in barracks without the others, and it's hard doing jobs with one arm out of action. The others have gone on with the rest of the legion, mopping up the enemy in the east and clearing up the mess they've left behind. Anyway, I can't train because of my wounded arm, so I get plenty of chances to go out to Ena's village.

I'm teaching her some more Latin, which

should come in handy now Britain is going be a part of the Roman Empire forever. Her dad wanted to know how long I was going to be in the army and when he understood I'd signed up for twenty-five years he raised his eyebrows. I tried to impress him by telling him that when I retire I'll get a big payment or some farmland of my own. Then I'll be able to marry officially and any children I've had will become Roman citizens. I don't think he understood all that, though.

He let me ramble on for a while, then looked me up and down, grunted and walked away. Ena and I burst out laughing. Celts and Romans still have a lot to learn about each other! But at least we've made a start.

December 1st AD60

This morning I was standing at one of the gates on sentry duty when I saw the flash of sunlight on metal in the distance. Then I heard the familiar sound of marching feet and saw the standards held high and proud. They're back! My mates have returned.

Soon we were all sitting in the barrack room, just like old times.

"What have you been up to, Marcus?" asked Felix. "I heard you've been working on our relations with the locals." They laughed and then they all started to tease me about my British girlfriend. I reckon they'd been working out different ways to do it all the time they've been away.

I was more interested in their news because I wanted to write it down in my diary. This is roughly what they told me:

NOT LONG AFTER THE BATTLE BOUDICCA DIED. SHE MIGHT HAVE KILLED HERSELF BUT NO ONE KNOWS FOR SURE, OR NOBODY'S SAYING. THE SECOND AUGUSTA LEGION DIDN'T TURN UP TO HELP US IN THE BATTLE BECAUSE THEIR COMMANDER DISOBEYED HIS ORDERS AND DECIDED THEY DIDN'T NEED TO BOTHER. HE PROBABLY DIDN'T REALISE HOW BIG THE CELTIC ARMY WAS.

ANYWAY, WHEN HE FOUND OUT WHAT HAD HAPPENED HE KILLED HIMSELF BY FALLING ON HIS OWN SWORD, BECAUSE HE HAD SHAMED HIS MEN.

MEANWHILE OUR LEGION IS COVERED IN GLORY AND WE SHOULD BE GETTING EVERY HONOUR GOING, BY THE SOUND OF IT. SUETONIUS PAULLINUS IS THE HERO OF THE HOUR AND SHOULD BE IN GREAT FAVOUR WITH THE EMPEROR BACK IN ROME.

AFTER THE BATTLE OUR SOLDIERS MARCHED EAST TO THE REBEL LANDS AND DESTROYED WHAT WAS LEFT (FARMS, WARRIOR BASES AND PLACES OF WORSHIP). LUCIUS SAID THERE WERE HARDLY ANY PEOPLE LEFT, ANYWAY, BECAUSE A LOT OF THEM HAD GONE OFF TO THE BATTLE, NEVER TO RETURN. THOSE THAT STAYED AT HOME MAY STARVE UNLESS WE HELP THEM BECAUSE THEY HAVEN'T SOWN A CROP THIS YEAR. APPARENTLY THEY WERE SO CERTAIN OF WINNING THEY THOUGHT THEY'D USE OUR GRAIN STORES AFTER THEY'D KILLED US ALL! I SHOULDN'T THINK WE'LL BE IN A HURRY TO HELP THEM, FRANKLY.

Galerius brought me back a souvenir, a small cooking pot he'd picked up from some ruined homestead. Trust Galerius to think about food.

"The rebel Celts have gone. Now we're in charge," said Gaius, yawning. "We are sole masters of a boggy puddle called Britain that fills with rain every day. You, Marcus, appear to like it. Me, I'm going to have to put up with it," he sighed and he settled down in his bunk. "Tell me, has Ena got any nice friends?"

I've missed Galerius's cooking very much and begged him to rustle me up a little something before he went to bed. Just a honey omelette would do.

"A tired cook is a bad cook," he said. "But I'll tell you what. Tomorrow I'll make you my special – boiled chicken with anchovy sauce." With that promise his head disappeared beneath his cloak.

"Nice to see you again, Marcus. Now we're a team again," smiled Felix. "Oh, and Pallo would send his love but I should think he's too busy aiming kicks at the fortress stable master."

Just then a head appeared around the barrack room door.

"Gallo. You've been having an easy time of it I hear," said Sejanus gruffly. "Your arm looks all right to me. Extra training for you, or you'll be getting flabby."

So here I am, with all my mates fast asleep around me, sitting here writing my diary in the lamplight.

I find it quite amazing to think how much has happened to me in the short time I've been in Britain. I've helped conquer a new land, met a special girl, and got a new scar or two. I've made some true friends and I've even got used to the rain trickling down my helmet.

But there's one thing I'll never get used to...

THEY'RE SNORING AGAIN!

WHERE DID IT HAPPEN?

This map of Britain shows the places Marcus has mentioned in his diary.

ANGLESEY (MONA)

POSSIBLE BATTLE SITE

CHESTER (DEVA)

WATLING STREET

COLCHESTER (CAMULODUNUM)

ST ALBANS (VERULAMIUM)

LONDON (LONDINIUM)

EXETER (ISCA)

FRANCE (GAUL)

Camulodunum, the Roman veteran soldiers' town destroyed by the rebels, was rebuilt and became Colchester. Londinium became London and Verulamium became St Albans. Archaeologists have dug down below the modern buildings in these towns and found layers of burnt material that mark the time when the Celts attacked and set fire to everything.

Skulls from this time have been found in the River Walbrook that once ran through the City of London. It's thought these might have been the heads of townspeople murdered by the rebels. They might have thrown the heads into the water as an offering to their gods. We do know that they looted the big bronze statue of the Emperor Claudius from Colchester and threw the head of the statue into the River Alde in Suffolk.

The Second Augusta Legion, which didn't turn up for battle, were based in Isca, now Exeter. Nobody knows for sure where the big battle between the legions and the rebels was fought, though it would have been somewhere along the Roman road called Watling Street. Some historians think it could have been at a place called Mancetter in Warwickshire.

The rebel tribes lived in Norfolk and Suffolk. Mona became Anglesey. Deva became Chester.

BURIED TREASURE

In East Anglia, part of Boudicca's old kingdom, treasure hoards of coins and precious metal objects have been dug up that date from this time. Local people may have buried their wealth to save it from the Romans. Perhaps they buried it before they went off to battle, expecting to dig it up later. They buried their coins in pots. Historians can date the burials by looking at the decoration on the coins, which are often Roman ones mixed with local ones. Roman coins of that time had the head of the Emperor Nero on them.

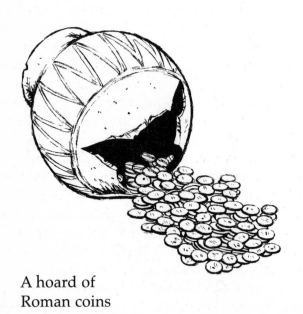

A hoard of
Roman coins

WHAT HAPPENED TO THE ROMANS?

The Romans ruled the southern part of Britain
for four hundred years. They ruled in Scotland
for a very short time; they never ruled in Ireland.

It was mostly a peaceful reign, although there
was sometimes trouble on the borders, especially
the ones facing Scotland. Eventually the Romans
built Hadrian's Wall to keep the non-Roman
tribes out of Roman-ruled areas.

Many Roman soldiers stayed on in Britain
after they left the army. When they retired they
were given a big payment, money that their
signifier had saved for them out of their wages.
If they preferred they could be given some land,
settle down and maybe even marry a local girl.

ALL ABOUT EMPERORS

Back in Rome things were anything but peaceful. It was just as well that Marcus and his friends were far away!

Nero was Emperor during the Boudiccan revolt. He reigned from AD54 to AD68 but during his life he became more and more insane. Eventually he behaved so badly that his own army guards, the Praetorians, decided to get rid of him. He committed suicide before they managed to kill him.

In the following year there were three emperors, all of them weak. Two of them were murdered and one committed suicide.

Eventually a new emperor, Vespasian, took control. He had served as a high-ranking soldier in Britain in AD53, and had won many battles around the Empire. He was a sensible ruler.

WHY DID THE ROMAN EMPIRE FALL?

By AD400 the Roman Empire had got too big. Its soldiers were sent far and wide, and over the centuries its best soldiers settled in the new lands, many miles away from Rome.

The emperors gradually grew weaker and more corrupt, and the ruling families of Rome spent most of the time squabbling among themselves. In the end there were no rulers or soldiers left strong enough to defend Rome itself, and the city was invaded by pagan enemies.

The Roman Army left Britain in AD410, recalled to fight in their homeland. Soon afterwards new invaders arrived in Britain from other parts of Europe. They were known as the Anglo-Saxons.

If you ever go to see the Roman remains at Chester you might hear the legend of 'the last sentry'. His ghost is said to appear at one of the gates of the old fortress. The story goes that when the Roman Army was finally ordered from Britain the soldiers drew lots to decide who would be the last legionaries, the ones who would stay and bravely guard the fortress gates until the barbarians finally invaded and killed them. The ghost is said to be one of these sentries.

GLOSSARY

Here are some Roman words explained to help you understand more about life in Roman times.

AMPHITHEATRE

An oval-shaped Roman sports stadium. In Rome there was a gigantic amphitheatre called the Colosseum, where thousands of people went to watch gladiator fights or wild animal hunts. In the intervals, prisoners were executed.

ARMOUR

A Roman legionary would wear a linen undershirt and a woollen tunic. On top of that he would wear the *lorica segmentata*, flexible armour which was made of metal strips joined together. He had hobnailed leather sandals called *caligae* and a helmet called a *galae* which protected him from blows to the head, neck and jaw. He had a curved shield called a *scutum* and a waistband called a *cingulum*. He had a *pilum* (javelin), a *gladius* (sword) and a *pugio* (dagger). He would also have had a military cloak called a *segum*.

In cold places, such as Britain, soldiers were allowed underwear and socks.

AQUILA

The most important standard of the legion. It filled the soldiers with pride when they saw it. It had an eagle on top (*aquila* is Latin for eagle).

AUXILIARIES

These were soldiers who were not Roman citizens. We know that some British Celts joined up and became auxiliaries during the Roman era. Auxiliaries looked different from legionaries. They had oval-shaped shields and a different uniform.

BOUDICCA

The Queen of the Iceni tribe. She led them in a rebellion against Roman rule.

CAVALRY

Auxiliary soldiers often had special horse-riding skills so they were put in cavalry units.

CENTURION

A senior soldier in charge of a century (eighty men). Centurions were responsible for training their men and for discipline too. They carried a large vine stock (a big stick) to hit soldiers who disobeyed them.

COHORT

A group of six centuries - 480 men, except for the First Cohort, which had 800 of the best troops. Every legion had ten cohorts.

Conturbenium

Eight soldiers who shared a barrack room.

Denarius

A Roman coin. Ordinary legionaries in the first century AD got about 225 denarii per year, which was good pay for the time. But a large part of their pay was kept back for equipment, food, savings and funeral expenses. Every four months or so they got pocket money of about thirteen denarii to spend.

Emperor

The ruler of the Roman Empire. It sounds like a good job! But lots of emperors got murdered, often by the Praetorian Guard, the Emperor's personal bodyguard.
Women weren't allowed to be emperors, but as the Emperor's wife or mother they could be very powerful.

Fort

There were different types of Roman fort. Fortresses were the largest, built to house a whole Legion or several cohorts. Forts were smaller, for one cohort, perhaps.
A marching camp was just a simple structure built for an overnight stop.

GODS AND GODDESSES

The Romans worshipped lots of gods and goddesses that lived in the underworld, on the Earth, in the sea or on Mount Olympus, in the sky. The King of the gods was Jupiter, who controlled the weather on Earth. The Queen of the gods was Juno, who ruled women and marriage.

LATIN

Here is the Latin alphabet. Try writing your name using the letters. Latin uses an I for a modern J, and a V for a modern U.

LEGATE

The man in charge of a legion – the equivalent of a modern general. Britain had an even grander version, a provincial legate, in charge of the whole country.

SENATORS

The top politicians of Rome. They came from important families and had to be rich. They sat in a kind of parliament called the Senate. The sons of senators usually served time as a tribune, a senior officer in the Roman Army.

SIGNIFIER

Signifiers carried the legions' standards into battle. They also looked after the soldiers' pay chests and savings. Their uniform included a bearskin.

STANDARDS

Poles with various symbols of the legion on them. They were the equivalent of regimental flags and every century had one. They were very important to the pride of the legion. If they were lost in battle it was considered a disaster.

VETERANS

Soldiers who had been in the army for twenty-five years could retire, often at the age of forty-five. Many veterans chose to settle close to the fortress where they had served as a soldier. Although legionaries couldn't marry they often had girlfriends and children living near their fortress. When they retired they were free to marry and their children became Roman citizens.

VICUS

The civilian settlement just outside a fortress. Legionaries' girlfriends and children might live here, along with local people who worked at the fortress. This is where soldiers came when they had time off. There might be a tavern and some shops there.

WATLING STREET

The Roman road that led from London up through the Midlands.

MARCUS'S SECRET CODE - PAGE 49

Read his message backwards, then put in new word breaks.

Other Titles in this Series

The Diary of a Young Tudor Lady-in-Waiting

Young Rebecca Swann is joining her aunt as a lady-in-waiting at the court of Queen Elizabeth the First. In her secret journal, Rebecca records how she learns to be a courtier, falls in love and uncovers a plot against the Queen. Read her diary and find out what life was *really* like for a young Tudor lady-in-waiting.

The Diary of a Victorian Apprentice

Young Samuel Cobbett is very excited – he is to be an apprentice at a factory making steam locomotives. Away from the shop floor, Samuel records in his diary how he learns his trade, falls in love and experiences accidents and danger. Read his diary and find out what life was *really* like for a Victorian apprentice.

The Diary of a Young Nurse in World War II

Young Jean Harris has just been hired to train as a nurse in a large London hospital. As Britain goes to war, Jean records in her diary how she copes with bandages and bedpans, falls in love and bravely faces the horrors of the Blitz. Read her diary and find out what life was *really* like for a young nurse on the Home Front in World War II.